I Like to Say Yes

Story by: Vicki Mayfield Camacho

Graphics and Illustrations by: Shatasia Jordan

Archway Publishing books may be ordered through booksellers or by contacting:

Archway Publishing
1663 Liberty Drive
Bloomington, IN 47403
www.archwaypublishing.com
1 (888) 242-5904

Because of the dynamic nature of the Internet, any web addresses or links contained in this book may have changed since publication and may no longer be valid. The views expressed in this work are solely those of the author and do not necessarily reflect the views of the publisher, and the publisher hereby disclaims any responsibility for them.

Any people depicted in stock imagery provided by Thinkstock are models, and such images are being used for illustrative purposes only.
Certain stock imagery © Thinkstock.

ISBN: 978-1-4808-5042-2 (sc)
ISBN: 978-1-4808-5041-5 (e)

Print information available on the last page.

Archway Publishing rev. date: 03/05/2018

This book is dedicated to my daughter Leslie, my son-in-law, Xavier and the Bright Morning Star Daycare in Bridgeport, Connecticut

Special thanks to whoisrealtoraddy.com

Do you love Mommy?

Yes!

Do you love Daddy?

Yes!

Yes! Yes! Yes!

I Like to say yes!

Do you like ice cream?

Yes!

Do you like cake?

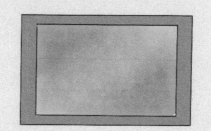

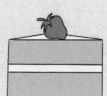
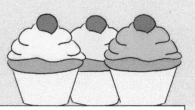

Yes!

Yes! Yes! Yes!

I like to say yes!

Do you like going to
the playground?

Yes!

Do you like to swing
on a swing?

Yes!

Do you like sliding
down the slide?

Yes!

Do you like riding in the car?

Yes!

Do you like running
really fast?

Yes!

Yes! Yes! Yes!

I like to say yes!

Endorsements

"[I Like to Say Yes] is really nice. I know that the children will enjoy the illustrations, and the message could not be more positive."

David Cohen director, Selma Maisel Nursery School, Temple Sholom, Greenwich, CT

"This book is dedicated to all parents of toddlers who only like to say no."

Miss Leslie Addy, former head teacher, Little Friends Child Care, Toddlers1, Greenwich, CT.

"The children really enjoy the book"

Ms. Malaysia Goodson, preschool Teacher, Toddlers1, Bright Morning Star, Bridgeport, CT

Author Biography

Vicki Mayfield Camacho is a former preschool teacher, a Home Visitor (A Home Visitor is a mobile preschool teacher) and mentor, in addition to being a play and screen writer, columnist and published author. She is the mother of an adult daughter, Leslie, and currently resides in Bridgeport, Connecticut. I Like to Say Yes is her first children's book.

CPSIA information can be obtained
at www.ICGtesting.com
Printed in the USA
BVHW061446020620
580778BV00005B/282

9 781480 850422